This ROARSOME book belongs to:

....

....

90710 000 554 234

A TEMPLAR BOOK

This book is based on the episode *Crying Wolfasaurus*
from the TV series *Gigantosaurus*™. Screenplay by Charles Henri Moarbes.
The TV series *Gigantosaurus*™ is created and produced by Cyber Group Studios.
Based on the original characters created by Jonny Duddle in the book *Gigantosaurus*,
first published by Templar Books in 2014.

First published in the UK in 2023 by Templar Books,
an imprint of Bonnier Books UK
4th Floor, Victoria House,
Bloomsbury Square, London WC1B 4DA
Owned by Bonnier Books
Sveavägen 56, Stockholm, Sweden
www.bonnierbooks.co.uk

Copyright © 2022 by Cyber Group Studios

1 3 5 7 9 10 8 6 4 2

ISBN 978-1-80078-233-4

Adapted by Samuel Fern
Edited by Harriet Paul and Kirsty Davison
Designed by Wendy Bartlet
Additional design by Ted Jennings
Production by Ché Creasey

Printed in China

FSC
www.fsc.org

MIX
Paper from
responsible sources
FSC® C104723

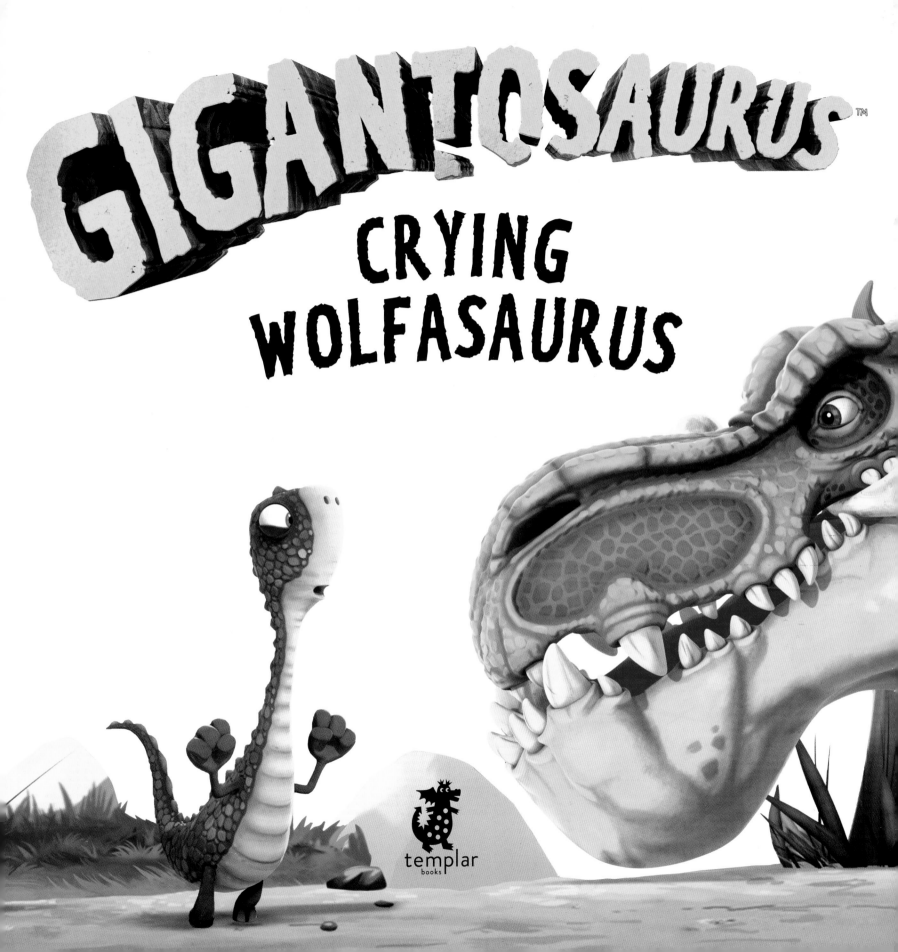

GIGANTOSAURUS™

CRYING WOLFASAURUS

templar books

"Are we nearly there yet?" Bill groaned, as he struggled to carry a huge picnic basket up the mountain. The little dinos were on a hike to the lookout.

"Why did you bring so much food?" Mazu called back. "We're only going for a picnic, not to live there forever!"

But just then, the jungle began to RUMBLE . . .

ROOOOAAAAR!

"GIGANTO!" Bill cried, hiding in his picnic basket.
His friends laughed as Giganto stomped past without a second glance.
Bill scowled. "My legs are shaking so much, I don't think I can walk . . ."

So Mazu, Rocky and Tiny had to carry Bill (and his enormous picnic) for the rest of the hike. It was hot work, but Bill didn't mind . . .

The only thing better than being surrounded by food . . . is being CARRIED while surrounded by food!

At last they arrived at the base of the lookout, and Rocky rigged a vine to the top.

Bill looked up in horror. "We're going to CLIMB?!"

"Come on, Bill," said Mazu. "It'll be worth it!"

Bill gazed hungrily at the food. "Let's just eat here."

Suddenly there was a loud THUMP and Bill shrieked,

"GIGANTOSAURUS!"

The other dinos leapt in fright, and the rope SNAPPED in Rocky's hands . . .

. . . But it was just little Rugo trying to crack open a nut with a gigantic stick!

"I'm sorry. There's no way up to the lookout now," Rocky said, sadly.

Mazu sighed. "We'll just have to picnic here instead."

But when they turned back to their feast, Bill was gobbling down the last berry!

"Bill!" Rocky cried. "That lunch was meant to be for all of us! What are we going to eat now?"

But before Bill could respond . . .

"GIGANTO'S COMING!" called a shrill voice.

Bill whirled around to see Rugo shouting, but there was no Giganto in sight! "What are you doing, Rugo?" he asked.

"Well, you cried 'GIGANTO' and got the snack you wanted, so I thought it might help me get this walnut open."

As Rugo ran off to find another way to open his walnut, Bill wondered whether Rugo was on to something.

Later, when the little dinos
were playing hide-and-seek . . .

1 . . . 2 . . . 3 . . .

AH-HA!
OH . . .

and Bill couldn't find his friends . . .

he decided to test
Rugo's theory.

He found a heavy rock, and THREW it
down on the dusty ground.

THUMP went the rock!

GIGANTO'S COMING!

In a flash, his friends ran
out of their hiding places.
"Found you!" Bill said, smugly.
"That's not fair!" Rocky scowled.
"You said Giganto was coming!"

Next, the little dinos went to the hot springs.
"It will be nice to warm my tired toes," said Bill.
But when they got there, the springs were full!

Bill grabbed the nearest boulder, slammed it down and cried, "GIGANTO'S COMING!"
In an instant, the springs were empty and Bill was lounging in the pool. His friends
were not impressed and glared at him as he relaxed in the hot water.

Later, the little dinos were playing a game of vineball.
Tiny was in goal, and no one could get a ball past her.

When it was Bill's turn to take a shot at goal, he rolled
his vineball into position, drew his leg back, and shouted . . .

GIGANTO'S
BEHIND YOU!

Tiny span around to look, and Bill's ball went sailing past her.
"GOAL!" yelled Bill, doing a victory dance.

"That's not fair!" Tiny cried. "You can't keep tricking us to get what you want!"
Before Bill could reply, Archie flapped in from the sidelines.
"Now, don't fight," he said. "It sounds like you could all do with
a night out at the archaeopera."

Archaeopera?
What's that?

It's when we gather together to sing around the lake!

"In the dark?" Bill asked. He wasn't sure about this but his friends all seemed keen to go. So . . .

"GIGANTO'S COMING!" he shouted, pointing behind them all. But Bill's friends had run out of patience with his tricks.

"But if it's dark, Giganto could stomp right over us!" Bill said, desperately.

Mazu crossed her arms. "Even in the dark, we'd hear him coming."
"Come on, let's go," said Rocky, leaving Bill to go home on his own.

"Places, everyone!" Archie called.

As Archie waved his baton, the gathered dinos moved to their places and
the fish released shining bubbles into the evening air.

"Now, Termy, let's check those drums!" Archie commanded.

Out in the lake, Termy let her rhythm loose on huge lily pad cymbals.

Back at the den, Bill was staring grumpily out of the window when who should silently pad across the savannah? Giganto!
"How is he walking so quietly?" Bill wondered.
Then he realised – Giganto was heading right towards the lake!

The sun was down and the archaeopera was in full swing when Bill arrived.
"Giganto . . ." he panted. "He's on his way!"

But before Bill could say anything more . . .

ROOOOAAAAR!

Giganto thundered out of the jungle, making the ground shake so much that Tiny, Mazu and Rocky were flung into the lake, landing on Termy's cymbals with a CRASH! "You broke my cymbals!" Termy shouted, looming over them.

I'm going to get you for this!

"I'll save you!" Bill called, leaping onto a floating bubble.

"Hurry!" Tiny cried, as Termy's toothy jaws got closer and closer.

Just then, Bill had an idea. He flew in close to Termy's ear and shouted . . .

Termy shrieked and swiftly swam off to the bottom of the lake.
"I'm so sorry," Bill apologised, once his friends were safely back on the beach.

We forgive you!

"But THAT is the ONLY time you can ever cry 'GIGANTO'!" laughed Tiny, and
the friends set off home to their warm and cosy den, together again.